Mariana
the Goldilocks
Fairy

by Daisy Meadows

Join the **Rainbow Magic Reading Challenge!**

Read the story and collect your fairy points to climb the Reading Rainbow online. Turn to the back of the book for details!

This book is worth 5 points.

The Fairyland Palace

Fairyland Library

The Three Bears' Cottage

Island

Thumbelina's Cottage

Storybook World

Rapunzel's Tower

Red Riding Hood's Grandmother's House

Red Riding Hood Woods

Mariana
the Goldilocks
Fairy

To baby bears everywhere, from the fairies

Special thanks to
Rachel Elliot

ORCHARD BOOKS

First published in Great Britain in 2016 by The Watts Publishing Group

A CIP catalogue record for this book is available from the British Library.

ISBN 978 1 40834 891 8

Printed and bound by CPI Group (UK) Ltd, Croydon, CR0 4YY

Orchard Books
An imprint of Hachette Children's Group
Part of The Watts Publishing Group Limited
Carmelite House, 50 Victoria Embankment, London EC4Y 0DZ

An Hachette UK Company
www.hachette.co.uk
www.hachettechildrens.co.uk

Jack Frost's Spell

The fairies want stories to stay just the same.
But I've planned a funny and mischievous game.
I'll change all their tales without further ado,
By adding some tricks and a goblin or two!

The four magic stories will soon be improved
When everything soppy and sweet is removed.
Their daft happy endings are ruined and lost,
For no one's as clever as handsome Jack Frost!

Contents

Puppet Problems

Kirsty Tate was walking along the river path towards the Story Barge, feeling thrilled to her fingertips. She loved books, and the Wetherbury Storytelling Festival was like a dream come true for her. Even better, she was enjoying every moment with her best friend, Rachel Walker, who was staying for the whole weekend.

"This day just gets better and better," said Rachel, slipping her arm through Kirsty's. "The Storybook Picnic was amazing, and now we're going to see a puppet show put on by Alana Yarn. I can't wait!"

Alana Yarn was one of their favourite authors. She was running the festival, which was being held in Wetherbury Park. The girls were attending every event they could. They had just come from a giant picnic, where they had eaten food inspired by their favourite stories. There had even been a cake in the shape of a very large storybook.

"What was your favourite food at the picnic?" Kirsty asked as they reached the Story Barge.

"I can't decide," said Rachel after a

moment's pause. "I loved the *Alice in Wonderland* 'Eat Me' cupcakes, but the *Peter Pan* fairy cakes were delicious too."

They were standing next to the Story Barge now, and there was a sign on the path advertising the show.

Alana Yarn's Puppet Show
Come along and guess the story!

"Come on!" said Kirsty.

She stepped on board the creaky old Story Barge. A short ladder led to the upper deck, which was piled with books. Inviting armchairs were dotted around, as well as plump floor cushions. Lots of children were already on board, looking very excited.

"Let's find a seat," said Rachel. "I want to look at all these books."

The girls settled down on a large blue cushion, and they were soon sharing a book that they had been longing to read.

Just as they finished the first chapter and exchanged happy grins, a head popped up from the wooden staircase that led down to the lower deck of the barge. It was Alana Yarn.

"The puppet show is ready," she announced. "Come on down to the lower deck, everyone. A story is waiting for you!"

The children made their way
downstairs and gathered on a large,
shaggy rug in the middle of the lower
deck. At the far end of the deck, Rachel
and Kirsty saw a small stage with a tall,
stripy puppet theatre and a large trunk.
The trunk had a curved lid, decorated
with pictures of fairytale characters.
Alana was standing behind the trunk,

and as soon as all the children were sitting down, she lifted the lid.

"I'd like you to try to guess what story I'm going to tell," she told the listening children. "Look carefully at the puppets and see if you can work it out."

First, she took out a large hand puppet of a girl with long, blonde hair. Then she placed some props on the stage.

Rachel and Kirsty watched as she set out three beds — one big, one small and one medium-sized. Next, three chairs appeared — one big, one small and one medium-sized. Finally, Alana took out three porridge bowls and looked around with a smile.

"Any ideas?" she asked.

Almost all the children raised their hands, looking excited. Alana nodded at Rachel.

"I think the puppet show is going to be about Goldilocks," she said.

"Quite right," said Alana with a laugh. "Now, I wonder if the girl next to you can guess which puppets I will bring out of the trunk next?"

Kirsty laughed too.

"Of course," she said. "The three bears."

A puzzled look crossed Alana's face.

"No, that's not right," she said, sounding confused.

Rachel and Kirsty glanced at each other in surprise. If they weren't the three bears, what could the puppets be?

Alana reached into the trunk and pulled out three green puppets — complete with big feet, knobbly heads and long noses.

They were goblins!

Into the
Book World

The other children laughed as if Kirsty
should have known.

"How could you think it was bears?"
asked a little boy sitting nearby. "Your
friend just said that the story was
Goldilocks."

"Yes, *Goldilocks and the Three Bears*,"
Kirsty agreed.

"Don't be silly," said the boy. "Everyone knows that it's Goldilocks and the Three Goblins."

The other children nodded in agreement.

"It's my favourite story," the boy went on. "I love how the three naughty goblins make such a mess in the cottage."

"That's not what happens," said Kirsty.

But no one except Rachel was listening. The girls shot each other an anxious look. They knew exactly what was happening.

That morning, Rachel and

Kirsty had met Elle the Thumbelina Fairy. She had whisked them to Fairyland, where they had met the rest of the Storybook Fairies – Mariana the Goldilocks Fairy, Rosalie the Rapunzel Fairy and Ruth the Red Riding Hood Fairy. They were all very upset. Jack Frost and his goblins had stolen their magical objects, and their stories were in danger of being spoiled forever.

Whoever held the magical objects had control of the stories. The fairies always used their objects to make sure the stories went as they were supposed to, and ended well. But Jack Frost and the goblins wanted the stories to be all about them, so they were using the magical objects to go into the stories and change them.

The girls had already followed the
goblins into the story of Thumbelina, and
helped her to marry her flower prince.
But there were three more magical
objects still to find.

"I'm so happy that we were able to
help Elle get her magic thumb ring back
from the goblins this morning," Kirsty
whispered. "But it looks as if Mariana
the Goldilocks Fairy will need our help
too. Someone is inside the story right
now, changing the bears into goblins!"

"Before the story starts, would anyone
like to come up to the stage and look at
the puppets and props?" Alana asked.

The children sprang to their feet and
hurried across to the puppet theatre.
Everyone wanted to have a closer look
at the beautiful puppets. But Rachel and

Kirsty held back and stood next to the props table. They looked at each other worriedly.

"What shall we do?" asked Rachel. "It's obvious that there are goblins inside the story of Goldilocks right now. How can we stop them?"

Kirsty bit her lip. "The fairy dust in our lockets would take us to Fairyland, but we wouldn't know where to find the Storybook Fairies. Besides, we need to get into the story of Goldilocks, and I don't think our fairy dust can do that."

She rested her hand on the table and dislodged one of the porridge bowls with a clatter. She picked it up to replace it, and then Mariana the Goldilocks Fairy fluttered out from underneath! She was wearing a blue pinafore dress, and her red shoes perfectly matched the bow in her golden hair.

"Hurray, I found you!" Mariana exclaimed. "I wasn't sure if I'd be able to get you away from the other children. Quickly, we need to find a place to hide so we can talk."

"This way," said Rachel, darting behind the puppet theatre.

Kirsty followed her, with Mariana fluttering at her side. The other children were still crowding around the puppets, so no one noticed the girls slipping out of sight. When they were safely hidden behind the puppet theatre, the girls looked up at Mariana with eager smiles.

"We're so glad you're here," said Kirsty. "Something has happened to the Goldilocks story, and we think that the goblins must be inside it right now."

"They are," Mariana said at once.

"That's why I'm
here. They've
got my
magic
spoon,
which
means
that
they can
change
whatever
they want in
the story. It's a disaster! I have to find a
way to make the Goldilocks story go as
it's supposed to."

"Yes, with three bears, not three
goblins," said Rachel.

"Exactly," Mariana agreed. "Elle told
me how amazing you were this morning,

helping her to get her magical thumb ring back from the goblins. I was hoping that you might be able to help me too?"

"Of course we will," said Kirsty at once. "We can't allow Jack Frost and his goblins to spoil the best stories in the world."

A smile spread across Mariana's face and she pulled a tiny book from inside her pinafore. She held it out to the girls, and they leaned closer.

The title was written in tiny, golden letters: *Goldilocks*. Mariana opened the book. The writing was so small that Rachel and Kirsty couldn't read it. But Mariana tapped the page with her wand, and a twist of golden sparkles spun out of the book. The twist grew bigger, until it swept the girls up, and all they could see was the glimmer of gold. They heard Mariana's voice above the whoosh of the swirling fairy dust.

"The Goldilocks story needs magic repairs.

We must stop the goblins and find the three bears.

Together I know we can quickly succeed,

And the goblins will feel very foolish indeed!"

Bear
Trackers

Gasping, the girls landed in a pile of
leaves. They looked around and saw that
they were just outside the white fence of
a little cottage, surrounded by a wood.
They could hear birds twittering among
the branches, and fluffy white clouds
floated overhead.

"It all seems very peaceful," said
Rachel, feeling puzzled. "I thought
that the goblins would be here already,
causing mischief."

Suddenly, the door
of the cottage
banged open, and
a little girl with
blonde ringlets
burst out. She ran
down the garden
path and slammed
the gate behind her.

"Are you all
right?" asked Kirsty, as she and Rachel
scrambled to their feet.

"I hope you're not going into the
cottage," said the girl, panting. "It's an
absolute mess! I couldn't wait to get out

of there – it's absolutely horrid!"

"Wait, are you Goldilocks?" asked Rachel. "Aren't you supposed to be inside the cottage, testing out the chairs and the beds?"

"I'm not going to sit on any chairs or lie on any beds in there," said Goldilocks. "It's filthy!"

She tossed her ringlets and ran off into the woods. Rachel and Kirsty exchanged worried glances.

"Come on," said Mariana. "We have to find out what's going on in there."

She fluttered over the gate, and the girls hurried up the path. Goldilocks had left the door swinging open on its hinges, and Rachel gave a loud knock and waited. No one came to the door.

"Oh dear, Goldilocks was right," said Kirsty, peering in through the doorway. "It's in a terrible mess."

They stepped into the cottage. The front door led straight into the kitchen, which was in uproar. Every single pot, pan and plate seemed to be on the floor. Pieces of broken china were scattered around, and all the cupboard doors were open. Someone had burst a bag of flour, coating everything in white powder. Tomato sauce had been squirted onto the table as if someone had used it to draw pictures. The kitchen taps were running, and the sink was about to overflow. Rachel darted over and turned the taps off.

"This is awful," said Mariana. "The three bears usually keep this cottage spick and span. I can't believe that they would leave it in this state."

"I'm sure they didn't," said Rachel, pointing to the floor. "Look – I think the goblins have been here."

There were large, muddy footprints all over the kitchen tiles.

"Those are definitely goblin prints," said Kirsty. "But they're not here now."

Rachel stepped back outside the cottage, gazing down at the path.

"There are more prints here," she said.

"Let's follow them," said Kirsty at once. "If we can find the goblins, we might be able to get Mariana's magic spoon back."

"But these aren't goblin footprints," said

Rachel, kneeling down. "These are paw prints – big ones, medium-sized ones and little ones."

"The three bears!" cried Mariana at once. "It must be them. We have to follow them and find out what happened here."

Rachel stood up and followed the prints down the path.

"It looks as if they went into the wood," she said. "It might take us a long time to track them – bears will be able to move through the wood more quickly than us."

"Not if you can fly like me," said Mariana with a smile.

She waved her wand, and the air shimmered with magic as Rachel and Kirsty shrank to fairy size. Seconds later they were fluttering beside Mariana on gauzy wings.

"Let's go!"
said Kirsty.
"We have
to find
the bears
and find
out what the
goblins have
been doing."

The paw
prints led the
fairies towards the centre of the wood.
It grew darker as they went deeper, and
they were surrounded by strange noises.
Kirsty reached out her hand, and Rachel
squeezed it.

"I'm glad you're here," Kirsty
whispered. "This wood is a bit spooky!"

Rachel smiled at her, and then

Mariana let out
a squeak of
excitement.
"I see
them!" she
exclaimed.
"Look!"
They
were flying
towards
a huge,
thick oak
tree, which
looked strong and
ancient. Its branches
reached up so high that the fairies
couldn't see the top. On the branch
closest to the ground, a baby bear was
snuffling his little nose. A medium-sized

mother bear was
sitting on the
branch above, and
a few branches
further up was
a very big father
bear. They were
all trembling so
much that
the leaves
on the
tree were
shaking.

"What's wrong?" asked Mariana, rushing to the biggest bear.

"Don't be upset!" cried Kirsty, fluttering over to the mother bear.

"There's nothing to be afraid of," said Rachel, hovering beside the baby bear. "We're here to help. What's happened?"

Just Right!

"It's been so scary," said Mummy Bear, her voice shaking. "But the day started happily. We were playing in the woods, and it was such a sunny day that we decided to go home and pack a picnic for lunch."

"But when we got home, we heard a terrible racket inside our cottage," Daddy Bear went on.

"I peeked through the windows," said Baby Bear, "and I saw three scary green creatures inside. They were horrible! They had big feet and long noses, and really mean expressions."

Kirsty and Rachel exchanged a knowing glance. The goblins!

"They were making a terrible mess," said Daddy Bear. "We ran back into the woods to hide. We don't want any trouble. Why would they be so mean?"

"Because they're goblins," said Rachel with a sigh. "That's their idea of fun."

"I'm too scared to go back home," said Mummy Bear. "But we didn't pack our picnic, and Baby Bear is very hungry.

We don't know what to do!"

"We've just been to your cottage," said Kirsty. "It was a mess, but the goblins had gone. It's safe for you to go home."

"Besides, we'll come with you," Mariana added.

"And we know the goblins," said Rachel. "We won't let them scare you again."

"I don't know," said Mummy Bear.

But Baby Bear's tummy gave a big, hungry rumble, and he looked up at his parents.

"Please, let's go home," he said. "I want my tea!"

Soon, the three bears were hurrying through the woods, while the fairies fluttered beside them. But when they reached the cottage, they all stopped in dismay. There was a lot of noise coming from inside. They could hear bangs, crashes and high-pitched squawks. The goblins were back.

"I've changed my mind," said Baby
Bear, his voice wobbling. "I'm not hungry
after all."

"We'll just stay in the woods," Mummy
Bear added.

"We won't let the goblins drive you out
of your home," said Kirsty. "Wait here
and we will go and talk to them."

The bears retreated behind the nearest
tree, while the fairies flew over the fence.

"There's an open window here!" called
Mariana.

They flew into the kitchen and landed
on the draining board. The three goblins
had made even more mess than before,
but now they were sitting around the
table in front of three bowls of porridge.
They were all wearing blue dungarees
and straw hats.

"Yum yum!" said the smallest goblin.
"Porridge is the best!"

"Especially when it belongs to someone
else," added the medium-sized goblin
with a snigger.

They each took a spoonful of their
porridge.

"Ow!" shrieked the smallest goblin.
"Too ho-ho-hot!

"Yuck!" grumbled the biggest goblin.

"It's stone cold!"

But the medium-sized goblin said nothing at all. He was too busy tucking in to his porridge. Mariana took a step forward.

"Look!" she said suddenly. "The medium-sized goblin is using my magic spoon to eat his porridge!"

He kept spooning it into his mouth until the bowl was scraped clean. Then he leaned back and patted his tummy.

"Just right," he said in a smug voice.

"Perhaps he will forget to pick the spoon up," Kirsty whispered. "One of us could grab it."

But just then the goblin reached out a bony hand, picked up the spoon and licked it clean. Then he tucked it into the back pocket of his dungarees.

Disappointed, the fairies slipped out of sight behind a saucepan, and watched. The smallest goblin got up and walked over to the fireplace, where three chairs were gathered around the fire. He sat down in the smallest chair. The medium-sized goblin plonked himself down in the next chair, and the biggest goblin took the biggest chair.

"This chair is too little for me," the smallest goblin grumbled. "My bottom keeps getting stuck, and it's much too hard."

"Well this one is too big and squashy for me," the biggest goblin complained. "It's swallowing me up!"

Only the medium-sized goblin looked happy.

"This one is just right," he said. "I'm so

clever – I picked the best one."

"Oh is that so?" huffed the biggest goblin. "We'll see about that!"

He tipped the medium-sized goblin out of the chair and sat down in it himself. Squawking with fury, the other two goblins started to push and prod him, trying to get him to move.

"I should have the 'just right' chair!" wailed the smallest goblin. "I'm the little one!"

The medium-sized goblin sat on the lap of the biggest goblin and bounced up and down. They fell to the floor together, shouting and scratching at each other.

"This is our chance!" Rachel whispered.

Food Fight

The fairies flew across the room to try to take the spoon while the goblins were squabbling, but the goblins were rolling around the floor too quickly. Then the smallest goblin clambered onto the 'just right' chair, and the others let out yells of fury. The biggest goblin shoved him, and he fell to the floor with a loud thump.

"You're mean to me!" he wailed. "I'm not playing with you any more!"

He scrabbled away from them and raced upstairs, closely followed by the other two goblins.

Rachel, Kirsty and Mariana looked at each other.

"What shall we do now?" asked Mariana. "There's no way that we can take the spoon back – they're moving too fast."

"We have to keep trying," said Kirsty in a determined voice. "Come on!"

They zoomed up the stairs and into the bedroom at the top. Fluttering against the ceiling, they watched the goblins leap up and down on the biggest bed.

"Rubbish!" shouted the smallest goblin. "This one's got no bounce at all – it's much too soft!"

They all bounded onto the next bed along, which was medium-sized. As they jumped, the bed made a cracking sound.

"They're going to break it!" Rachel exclaimed.

"They don't care," said Mariana.

"Hopeless!" the biggest goblin squawked. "This bed is too hard. It's like trying to bounce on a piece of wood!"

They leapfrogged onto the last and smallest bed. Now they were so close together that their tummies were touching. But they had big smiles on their faces, and they all started to giggle.

"Wheeee!" squealed the medium-sized goblin. "This is just right!"

"Now's our chance," said Rachel as the goblins jumped higher and higher. "We have to fly up behind the goblin with the spoon, and take it out of his pocket before he spots us."

"It's very risky," said Mariana, turning pale.

Rachel and Kirsty seized her hands.

"Be brave, Mariana," said Kirsty. "We

can do it!"

The fairies flew across the ceiling to the curtains and then fluttered downwards behind them, keeping out of sight.

"Let's get under the bed and then fly up together," said Rachel. "Hopefully one of us will be able to take the spoon."

They swooped down under the biggest bed and the medium-sized bed towards the goblins. When they were under the smallest bed, Rachel held up three fingers and counted down, to make sure that they would all fly out at exactly the same moment. Three … two … one …

Whoosh! They zipped upwards, but just at that moment the smallest goblin jumped off the bed and spotted them.

"Fairies!" he yelled. "This place is infested with fairies! Run!"

All three goblins bounced off the bed and scurried downstairs to the kitchen. Rachel, Kirsty and Mariana followed them past the fireside chairs towards the kitchen table. The porridge bowls were still there, and two of them had hardly been touched. The goblins dived under the table.

"I've got an idea!" said Kirsty with a gasp. "Mariana, can you make us human-sized again? I think I know a way to make him take the spoon out of his pocket."

Mariana swished her wand through the

air, and instantly Rachel and Kirsty were girls again. Kirsty darted over to the table and picked up one of the spoons. Then she peered under the table.

"Come out of there!" she demanded.

The goblins scrambled out, staring at her in astonishment.

"How did you get there?" asked the biggest goblin.

"Where are the fairies?" asked the medium-sized goblin.

Kirsty didn't reply. She just scooped up a big spoonful of porridge, took a deep breath and catapulted it at the biggest goblin. Splat! It hit him square on the forehead.

"Porridge fight!" he squealed, sounding delighted.

He pulled the magic spoon out of his back pocket, dug it into the other bowl of porridge and flung a cold lump of it at Kirsty. The other goblins grabbed spoons and started to fling porridge too. Soon they had forgotten about the girls and were hurling cold porridge at each other. Kirsty and Rachel ducked behind an armchair as porridge flew over their heads and goblin shrieks filled the air. Mariana was hiding behind a curtain.

"At least the magic spoon is out of the goblin's pocket," said Rachel. "Now we have to get it back for Mariana!"

A lump of porridge hit the wall nearby and Kirsty winced.

"I know it was naughty to start a food fight," she said. "I just couldn't think of any other way to get the spoon back."

"You did the right thing," said Rachel. "We can clean up afterwards. Besides, I've got a plan …"

Three Goblins, Three Bears and a Picnic

The girls peeped out from behind the chair. There was porridge all over the kitchen. The walls were dripping, and the surfaces and floor were covered in slippery porridge puddles. Rachel took Kirsty's spoon, stood up and flung another blob of porridge at the biggest

goblin. Then she backed away towards
the stairs, followed by Kirsty.

"Come back here!" the goblin barked.

He tried to run after them, but skidded
in a porridge puddle and skated across
the floor with his arms flapping. The
magic spoon flew out of his hand.

"No!" shouted the other goblins.

They dived towards the magic spoon,
belly-flopping into the porridge, and
went sliding across the floor on their
tummies.

The magic spoon landed in Kirsty's hand, and the goblins groaned as her fingers closed around it. Flapping around in the porridge, they watched as Kirsty held out the spoon to Mariana. The little fairy fluttered out of her hiding place and took the spoon. It immediately shrank to fairy size, and glowed for a moment as if it were glad to be back in her hand. Mariana's eyes shone with happiness.

"Hurray!" cried Rachel, clapping her hands together.

"It's not fair!" wailed the smallest goblin.

Just then, there was a noise at the door. The girls looked up and saw the three bears peeping around the corner. They all looked nervous, but when they saw the goblins, their expressions changed. Their eyes crinkled at the corners, their mouths twitched, and then they started to laugh.

"Hee hee," said Mummy Bear, with her paw over her mouth. "Now that they're covered in porridge, they don't look scary any more."

"They just look silly!" added Baby Bear.

The goblins looked around. When they saw the big bears looming over them, they all squealed.

"Help!" shouted the biggest goblin.

"We're all going to be eaten!" wailed the medium-sized goblin.

"Run!" the smallest goblin shrieked.

The goblins dived out through the kitchen window, and the bears stepped into their home.

"Oh dear, look at this mess," said Mummy Bear with a groan.

"Don't worry," said Mariana, fluttering forwards.

She waved her wand, and the porridge disappeared from the walls, floors and surfaces. The pots and pans danced their way back into the cupboards, and soon everything was tidy and sparkling clean. In a final flurry of sparkles, a picnic basket appeared on the kitchen table.

"Honey sandwiches," said Mariana with a smile. "You must all be very hungry by now."

"Thank you!" said the bears in delight.

They picked up the picnic basket and set off into the wood, waving goodbye as they went. Mariana turned to the girls.

"How can I ever thank you?" she asked.

"There's no need," Rachel replied.

"Oh yes there is," said Mariana. "And

I know just the way! My porridge is
famous, and I am going to make a pot
for you – right now."

With a whispered spell and a wave of
her wand, a pot of porridge appeared on
the kitchen table. The aroma was mouth-
watering, and the girls could hardly wait
to try it.

"Delicious!" said Kirsty
when she took her
first mouthful.
"Not too hot
and not too
cold."

"Not
too salty
and not too
sweet," Rachel
added. "It's just right!"

69

When they had finished eating,
Mariana raised her wand.

"Time to go back to the human world,"
she said. "I will never forget your bravery
and kindness today. Thank you!"

As Mariana's wand swished and the
girls waved, they glimpsed someone
through the kitchen window. It was
Goldilocks, and she was walking up the
path towards the cottage.

"Everything is turning out as it should,"
said Kirsty, as the cottage melted away
around them.

Suddenly they were back on the Story
Barge, behind the stripy puppet theatre.
Not a moment had passed since they had
set off on their magical adventure. They
went back to join the other children, as
Alana Yarn clapped her hands together.

"All right, everyone, this puppet show needs volunteers!" she said. "Who would like to help me to tell this story?"

The other children hesitated, but Rachel stepped forwards. Alana smiled at her.

"Well done for being the first," she said. "I'd like you to operate the Goldilocks puppet."

Smiling from ear to ear, Rachel picked up her puppet.

"Now, I need volunteers to work the puppets for the three—" Rachel and Kirsty held their breath— "bears!"

Kirsty's hand shot into the air, and she was picked along with two other children.

"You can be Baby Bear," Alana told Kirsty. "Now, everyone else, take your seats. The show is about to begin!"

The puppet show went perfectly. At the end, when the three bears returned from their picnic to find Goldilocks in their cottage, Kirsty caught Rachel's eye and they exchanged a smile of relief. The story of *Goldilocks and the Three Bears* had been saved, and they couldn't wait to save the rest of the Storybook Fairies' stories!

Meet the
Stroybook Fairies

Elle
the Thumbelina
Fairy
The Storybook Fairies

Mariana
the Goldilocks
Fairy
The Storybook Fairies

Rosalie
the Rapunzel
Fairy
The Storybook Fairies

Ruth
the Red Riding Hood
Fairy
The Storybook Fairies

Can Rachel and Kirsty help get their new fairy friends'
magical objects back from Jack Frost, before all
their favourite stories are ruined?

www.rainbowmagicbooks.co.uk

Now it's time for Kirsty and
Rachel to help...

Rosalie the Rapunzel Fairy

Read on for a sneak peek...

"Hurry up, Kirsty," called Rachel Walker,
skipping past colourful bunting and
festival tents. "I can't wait to get to the
Story Barge."

Her best friend, Kirsty Tate, had paused
to look at a tent that was decorated with
the first lines of lots of different children's
books. She grinned at Rachel and ran to
catch her up.

"That tent is amazing," she said. "I
want to make sure I go back later and
see how many first lines I recognise."

Rachel and Kirsty were having a
wonderful weekend. Rachel was staying

with Kirsty so that they could go to the Wetherbury Storytelling Festival together. One of their favourite authors, Alana Yarn, was leading the festival and had arranged lots of fun storytelling activities.

"We did so much yesterday, it feels as if we've had a whole weekend already," said Rachel. "There was the *Goldilocks* puppet show and Alana's storytelling performance of *Thumbelina*."

"And we met the Storybook Fairies," Kirsty added, remembering the magical adventures they had shared with Elle the Thumbelina Fairy and Mariana the Goldilocks Fairy.

"And we've still got the whole of Sunday ahead of us," said Rachel, stopping to do a cartwheel. "I'm so excited! I wonder what Alana has planned for today."

"I hope we see the Storybook Fairies again," Kirsty added.

"I'm sure we will," said Rachel. "After all, there are two magical objects still to find."

The girls were secret friends of Fairyland, but this was the first time that they had met the Storybook Fairies. Elle the Thumbelina Fairy had asked Rachel and Kirsty to help them, because Jack Frost had stolen their magical objects.

Read **Rosalie the Rapunzel Fairy** to find out what adventures are in store for Kirsty and Rachel!

Calling all parents, carers and teachers!
The Rainbow Magic fairies are here to help
your child enter the magical world of reading.
Whatever reading stage they are at, there's
a Rainbow Magic book for everyone!
Here is Lydia the Reading Fairy's guide to
supporting your child's journey at all levels.

Starting Out

1 Our Rainbow Magic Beginner Readers are perfect for first-time readers who are just beginning to develop reading skills and confidence. Approved by teachers, they contain a full range of educational levelling, as well as lively full-colour illustrations.

Developing Readers

2 Rainbow Magic Early Readers contain longer stories and wider vocabulary for building stamina and growing confidence. These are adaptations of our most popular Rainbow Magic stories, specially developed for younger readers in conjunction with an Early Years reading consultant, with full-colour illustrations.

Going Solo

3 The Rainbow Magic chapter books - a mixture of series and one-off specials - contain accessible writing to encourage your child to venture into reading independently. These highly collectible and much-loved magical stories inspire a love of reading to last a lifetime.

www.rainbowmagicbooks.co.uk

"Rainbow Magic got my daughter reading chapter books. Great sparkly covers, cute fairies and traditional stories full of magic that she found impossible to put down" - Mother of Edie (6 years)

"Florence LOVES the Rainbow Magic books. She really enjoys reading now" Mother of Florence (6 years)

The Rainbow Magic Reading Challenge

Well done, fairy friend – you have completed the book!
This book was worth 5 points.

See how far you have climbed on the **Reading Rainbow**
on the Rainbow Magic website below.

The more books you read, the more points you will get,
and the closer you will be to becoming a Fairy Princess!

How to get your Reading Rainbow
1. Cut out the coin below
2. Go to the Rainbow Magic website
3. Download and print out your poster
4. Add your coin and climb up the Reading Rainbow!

There's all this and lots more at
www.rainbowmagicbooks.co.uk

You'll find activities, competitions, stories, a special
newsletter and complete profiles of all the
Rainbow Magic fairies. Find a fairy with your name!